I REALLY LIKE **MOM**

Mom, I love you
—S.L. and S.K.

The illustrations for this book were made digitally, with acrylic, etc.

Cataloging-in-Publication Data has been applied for
and may be obtained from the Library of Congress.

ISBN 978-1-4197-6824-8

난 엄마가 참 좋아 (I REALLY LIKE MOM)
Text © 2021 이수안 (Su-an Lee)
Illustrations © 2021 김소라 (So-ra Kim)
All rights reserved.

English translation © 2024 Paige Morris
Book design by Natalie Padberg Bartoo

First published in South Korea by BIR Publishing Co., Ltd. in 2021. This edition published in 2024 by Abrams Books for Young Readers, an imprint of ABRAMS. All rights reserved. No portion of this book may be reproduced, stored in a retrieval system, or transmitted in any form or by any means, mechanical, electronic, photocopying, recording, or otherwise, without written permission from the publisher.

Printed and bound in China
10 9 8 7 6 5 4 3 2 1

Abrams Books for Young Readers are available at special discounts when purchased in quantity for premiums and promotions as well as fundraising or educational use. Special editions can also be created to specification. For details, contact specialsales@abramsbooks.com or the address below.

Abrams® is a registered trademark of Harry N. Abrams, Inc.

ABRAMS The Art of Books
195 Broadway, New York, NY 10007
abramsbooks.com

I REALLY LIKE MOM

words by Su-an Lee | pictures by So-ra Kim
translated by Paige Morris

Abrams Books for Young Readers
New York

I really like Mom.
She's always there for me.

When I stretch myself awake in the mornings
and drift off to sleep on dark nights,
she's always by my side.

I really like Mom.

I really like Mom.
She makes me yummy food.

She whips up meals
that simmer in the pan
and help me grow big and strong.

I really like Mom.

I really like Mom.
She sings to me.

She *clap-clap-claps* her hands when she's excited and *swish-swishes* from side to side when she dances. She sings *la-la-la*, a song just for me.

I really like Mom.

I really like Mom.
She gives me kisses.

She smooches my cheeks,
mwah-mwah-mwah,
when we're splashing in the water
and listening to the wind whoosh by.

I really like Mom.

I really like Mom.
She gives me compliments.

She praises me for playing nicely with my friends as we take turns sharing my favorite toy.

I really like Mom.

I really like Mom.
She waits for me.

She waits until I'm all done playing in the leaves
and I've had my fill of the smells of the forest.

I really like Mom.

I really like Mom.
She holds my hand tight.

When my heart is pounding and I don't feel brave,
or I fumble and fall down,
she grabs my hand and squeezes.

I really like Mom.

That she treasures me
more than anything
and feels so happy just to be my mom.

I really like Mom.

I really like Mom.
She gives me hugs.

When I'm sick and coughing with a cold,
or I'm sad after my toy gets smashed to pieces,
she holds me close.

I really like Mom.

Tales of growling, prowling animals
and shining, shimmering stars.
Stories are so much fun when she reads them.

I really like Mom.